ZOMBIE ZERO
THE SHORT STORIES

THE HEART OF
THE MONSTER

Zombie Zero: The Short Stories
The Heart of the Monster

ISBN-13: 978-1-944916-86-2
ISBN-10: 1-944916-86-5

www.SuddenInsightPublishing.com
Indie publishing for the Indie Author

ZOMBIE ZERO
THE SHORT STORIES

THE HEART OF
THE MONSTER

J.K. NORRY

FOREWORD

If this is the first of my 'Year of the Zombie' books you have encountered, I hope you love these stories. The commentary in between is me talking to those readers who like a little something extra from the author. If you aren't one of those people, feel free to skip the commentary and go straight to the three short stories in this book. I would ask that you read this, and the afterword, and the recommendation I have for you after that; but you won't offend me if you just want the stories. If you love them, there are a lot more! There is also 'Zombie Zero: The First Zombie' and 'Zombie Zero: The Last Zombie', the two main books that these stories are built around. I sincerely hope that you read them all, and that you enjoy them a great deal.

If you already have read the other books, you know all this; you even know about the 'Secret Society of Deeper Meaning', and how much it means to me if you join up. Thanks for reading, if that's you! And thanks for joining up, if that's you!

If you haven't joined yet, you might think about it. There's more cool stuff coming next year than there was this year, and I think I see a pattern forming here...

Of course, you have a book in your hand; you should probably read it first of all. The commentary won't have any spoilers, that might ruin any of the other books or the stories; it's mostly me letting you know a little about writing and compiling these volumes. Being an author has brought me out of my shell in more ways than I had anticipated, and I am grateful for that in many ways. It surprised me to discover that some folks liked knowing more about me, and my motivation; it surprised me even more that I delighted in sharing.

In that spirit, I would like to tell you a short story from my life before we get on to the ones that came through my antennae. A big inspiration for this project were the pulp horror and science fiction publications that I gobbled up as a kid. That wasn't all, though; I also still love a meaningful short story.

I told you about a book I had, in the last volume; now I'd like to tell you about a story I read, how it affected me as a kid and how it came back around to affect me again later.

If I might...

ABOUT THE SHORT STORIES

Books have always been a big part of my life, and long stories have helped bring about pivotal changes in me more than once. A few short stories have done the same, and this is a true story about one of them. One of my favorite writers of short stories is Ray Bradbury. His long books are awesome too, but his short stories were my first introduction to this author. I'll do one of those things I only do when something is really meaningful to me, and mention another author's work in my book.

'The Pedestrian' is the name of the short story that I read, back then. It was in a collection, but that one really stood out for a number of reasons. I had a lot of questions when I was a kid. So many of them started with 'what if' that I was asked not to use the phrase to start any more sentences on more than one occasion. Bradbury's way of pointing out that things were super weird without using excessive profanity to do so intrigued me right away. It was some time later that the story hit home again.

After growing up in rural Montana, I headed out to Seattle to try the 'big city life'. Many of my childhood hopes and dreams were thankfully shattered there, and I was left to put together a reality deliberately of my own making. New hope rose from that dark night of my soul, where I spent months locked away from the world under internal construction. One of the simplest pieces of advice that I encountered in many of the non-fiction I had begun to read was that it's always good to go for a walk. It sounded like good advice; the rare moments of peace I had enjoyed in childhood were found deep in the woods on a trail worn by wildlife. Maybe I might pick up a bit of peace walking a city street too.

If you don't know the Puget Sound area, that's okay. We'll just say that Renton had some pretty bad neighborhoods back then, and that was the only place I could afford an apartment of my own. The internal work I was doing required that solitude, and I didn't mind spending most of what I was making to create that environment. Of course, I was down to free stuff when it came to finding a way to entertain myself. So I found myself going for a walk, rather late at night, trying to clear my head.

I had been walking for awhile, when it happened. A car pulled to the side of the road, blue and red lights flashing. Taking my hands from my pockets, I stopped and turned to face the police officer as he approached.

"Good evening," I said, pleasantly enough.

He grimaced a little, pointed out that it was later than that. Quite a bit later.

I said I couldn't sleep, and had decided to go for a walk. He grimaced again, replied that he had gotten reports of a suspicious character skulking about downtown. After looking myself over, I wondered aloud what was so suspicious about me. He felt obliged to point out the late hour once more.

"Have you been drinking?" he asked.

"I haven't indulged in any mind-altering substance for several months," I replied proudly. It was true, too; at the time. My first big experiment in self-exploration activated a lot of chemicals within me, but there was deliberately no outside stimuli involved. It was too much information to tell a police officer at three or four in the morning in downtown Renton, but it was true. It's probably even part of why he wanted to see my identification, and why I stood out there waiting to get it back for longer than I had planned on being out walking.

We finally got it all straightened out, though he never quite seemed to buy my 'I'm just out for a walk' story. He told me I ought to head on home, and I told him that was just what I had been thinking. There had been a few frightening moments there, where I wondered absurdly if I was doing or had done something illegal without even knowing about it. Considering the possibility that my freedom was in question made me long for that crappy little apartment that I had been trying to get away from.

I didn't think about Bradbury's story until I was nearly home. His pedestrian ends up going to jail, for the same act I had been committing. He had gone for a walk, a suspicious thing for a man to do in Bradbury's future world. I had done the same, and been accosted somewhat similarly. His story ended with the poor fellow being hauled off by an automated police car; thankfully my story ended up with me back home, thinking about his story for the first time in years.

Of course, Ray Bradbury was not the only person who influenced this series in one way or another. There are actually of couple of people that had a lot to do with the way this all came together, and that's what I'd like to tell you about next.

ODE TO SEAN HARRINGTON

When we first chose an artist for the 'Year of the Zombie' projects, there were only two books planned. As the short stories began to speak to me, and then take shape, it became apparent that we were going to have to get some more book covers. Since they were all outlined, I was able to say how many there would be; how to compile them was a different subject altogether. It soon became clear that the artist we had chosen should be part of the inspiration for how we did it, and that he should be given the option of coming up with six more covers on his own.

Sean Harrington nailed it, every time. The covers for these short stories were all his ideas, based on synopses that I sent him. The type of art that I had wanted for 'The First Zombie' and 'The Last Zombie' was perfectly suited for these collections, and he really knocks it out of the park with that stark pulp style. Giving him creative freedom was a great choice with these covers, although it was harder to wait for them without knowing just what we were waiting for.

Every time a new piece showed up, we did a lot of whooping and hollering and talking about how cool it was for several days to follow. It was also more exciting, not knowing exactly what to expect.

The art and stories from horror and science fiction pulp publications left a real impression on me. Writing these stories, knowing they would be compiled in relevant sets of three that would fit in someone's back pocket in the print version was extra cool. Even more cool would be to have a cover that related to the content, I supposed. Sean Harrington took that to the next level, and made the world of 'Zombie Zero' come alive in ways I hadn't anticipated. As much work as I put into this project, I knew I couldn't do it alone. It was something special to work with such a talented and professional artist in making this dream come true for me.

Thanks again, Sean Harrington! Your art brought something to my art that it wouldn't have had without you, and it has been a special honor to watch my stories take new shape at your hands.

Of course, that's not the only help I had in building up and tearing down the world of 'Zombie Zero'. I have a secret weapon, and I'm also terrible at keeping secrets.

ODE TO DAWN MARSHALL

My secret weapon has a name, and her name is Dawn Marshall. Pretty much everything I do is made possible in one way or another by her, and she deserves all the credit I can manage to send her way. Dawn is actually a wonderful example of gentle strength, and is not really best described as a weapon; and I talk about her all the time, so she's not really a secret either. She is the 'why' behind my 'what' whenever it's something worth doing, and she's a big part of the 'how' as well.

Dawn knows I am on the company Appletop for a bunch of reasons. She knows that I am pursuing my dream wholeheartedly, and she's there to do all the technical aspects of publishing each book as soon as I'm done writing it. She also knows that I'm working toward a future where I almost never have to leave home, and that she's the one that makes me want to be there all the time. Our purpose has become so intertwined that it becomes hard to imagine being so close without working together so closely.

Lucky for me, there's no need to imagine; the more we work together, the more smoothly everything flows.

Some say I'm a hard person to disagree with. Generally it's because I don't want to waste time listening to an idea that won't work when I have one that will. That's not the case with Dawn. I love when she disagrees with me; it's almost always an opportunity to do something better, or see something clearer, or look at things in an entirely new way. Those moments often lead to a whole new level of living for me, in one of the many areas of my life that depend so much on her. It means a lot to me to be able to say that, and even more to be able to live it.

From the outside, Dawn and I appear to be living a very busy and ever-changing life. It will always appear that way, I suspect. We both love the satisfaction of a job well done, we both have immense curiosity about life and all the places and things to explore, and a real need to make both ourselves and our partner happy. That may sound like a lot of work, unless those are things you love to do; then it just sounds like a great life, and a never-ending list of wonderful things to do.

Thanks, Dawn, for being such a perfect partner in all the things I love to do.

ABOUT FRANK'S PURPOSE

This was one of the glimpses I got, while writing 'The First Zombie', into the lives affected by the actions of the main characters. I found myself wondering, as one life touched another, where the other life was headed after their own dramatic paradigm shift. Answering that question became one of the many reasons that were piling up to write these short stories. It's no surprise that this was the second story I got started on, and the second that was completed as well. It was clear that they were meant to come in a certain order, at this point.

Figuring out that order was not the easiest part of this project, and I didn't really have it all properly sequenced until long after this set was done. We ending up releasing this story first to newsletter subscribers, for a number of reasons. One of those reasons is that I thought this would be the first set that would get compiled into print and ebook format. After outlining the rest of them, and writing more of them, it soon became apparent that I was wrong again.

The first three books that got released on the heels of 'The First Zombie' pretty obviously needed to come first. The timeline was represented way better that way, as these short stories all happen somewhere during that first larger book.

'The Sickness Spreads' implied that timeline with its title, and came out first. As the sickness did spread, it was also important to consider the tie-ins happening within these short story sets. Immediately after reading 'The First Zombie' and 'The Sickness Spreads', it made sense to read the stories in 'The Beginning of the End' next, followed by the set in 'Love Lost at Sea'. There were strong tie-ins and good timeline set-ups going on all the way through 'The Zombie Killers' and 'Monstrous Consequences' for the most part as well.

This one ended the series for a different reason. The events in these stories happen earlier in the book, starting with the big tie-in right away. That tie-in is in Chapter Nine of 'Zombie Zero: The First Zombie', and that's all I can really say without spoiling one story or the other. It's a different kind of story, and hopefully you'll soon see why I thought 'Frank's Purpose' was the best way to start the final set in this series.

FRANK'S PURPOSE

Frank drummed his fingers on the steering wheel, pressed a button on the device mounted to the dash. The screen lit up with an image of his wife and son, and numbers too small to read. Frank pressed the button again, and the numbers reappeared in larger form. Two more minutes, and his shift was over. So long as no one hopped in the back of the cab in the next one hundred twenty seconds, he was off to his home and his family.

Flipping down the visor, he looked at the other constant reminder of his love and his purpose. Maria was his love; little Juan was his purpose. He pressed the button on the device again, then once more. One more minute, and he could get home to Maria... Maria, and her kisses and her delicious dinners and her fresh flowery scent; he could carefully approach his son, and maybe even get a hug out of him. Probably not any eye contact, but maybe a hug.

The door opened, and someone got in the back.

Frank reached up to adjust the rearview, to get a look at the guy. A series of sharp bursts of pain exploded in his shoulder, and the only view he got was of the top of the man's head as he bit into Frank's shoulder.

He opened his mouth to cry out, instinctively. Before any sound could issue forth, a strange feeling swept over him. Frank closed his mouth, and smiled at the monster in the mirror.

A string of words in English spilled from the monster's mouth, too fast for him to catch them all or translate them. A clear image filled his head: a street with people, but not too many. Hunger twisted his belly, and Frank's thoughts dwindled to the simple mechanical responses required to slake that hunger. He knew where to go. After only a minute of driving, the creature spoke again; he pointed, and Frank did not need to understand his words to follow his direction.

Pulling the cab to the curb, Frank watched while the monster coaxed an older lady into the back with him. He saw the creature reach out with long claws that got caught up in her hair and wrench her violently forward. He watched his own hands grasp her from behind, to hold her and stop her from screaming. Frank noted with dull-witted hunger that his hands were different, as were the monster's.

When it had gotten in the cab, the monster had looked like a man whose flesh had been rotting off for a good long while. Now he looked like a creature made for killing: he had sprouted rows of sharp teeth from a skull that had grown thicker and wider; a narrow ridge ran along the top of its skull where his powerful biting muscles came together. All along his face, those thick strings of sinew were exposed, as his flesh had never grown back. He had grown claws that had turned his rotting hands into talons, and his arms had gotten leaner and longer. Three scant folds of flesh cut gory horizontal lines across his throat.

Frank looked at his own hands as he held the woman with his death grip. The flesh was already falling off of them in small dripping globules. He felt his face, hot with droplets of what used to be his somewhat handsome features. He felt the hunger, and envied the monster as it bit into the woman.

She pulled herself from his grasp, as strong as Frank. He watched her press herself into the monster, like a lover desperate for his touch. The creature was more powerful than both of them, and he shoved her off of him and out into the street. Frank met her eyes as she raised her head; they were a rusted red color, and shot with blood.

The monster called out to her, and turned to Frank.

"Go!" the creature cried. It's voice was the tangled mess of a shriek and a growl. Frank started at the sound, then put the cab in gear. He knew what that word meant.

A minute or two passed before the creature spoke again. Frank glanced in the mirror as they traversed a deserted stretch of lane slowly. His face was gone; his hunger was not. For some reason the only thought he had, even as he glanced at his own gruesomeness, was feeding. He couldn't remember who he was, or who he had been; and he had no reason to try. All Frank had anymore was hunger; all he was anymore was hunger. His every thought was of hunger, of flesh, of blood. It made no sense to his hunger when he took the photo from the visor and slipped it in his jacket pocket; it was just another mechanical motion.

The words the monster spoke were garbled unintelligibility to Frank; the mental image that followed was paradise. A man was standing on the side of the road, the only person in sight. In his mind, Frank saw an image of himself eating the man bit by delicious bit.

Frank cranked the wheel, jumped the curb and took the man out at the knees. He had the door open before the vehicle stopped, and barely had the presence of mind to go through the automatic motions of putting the car in neutral and setting the brake. Aching legs carried his twisting hunger around the fender, and Frank collapsed on the fallen pedestrian.

Clawing at him, biting at him, chewing on him, Frank felt his limbs grow long and powerful as his higher brain functions came back to him. Long rows of teeth sprouted in his mouth, sharp razored claws sprung from his fingertips, and he used the new tools to strip every last piece of flesh from the fallen corpse. For a moment, the man had fought; then he had embraced the feast; then he had died. Somewhere in all the chewing and changing Frank had felt the first monster's mind reach out to him, to learn about the city and the car's transmission; then he had lost himself in his hunger, and hardly noticed the cab pulling away.

Standing up, Frank looked down at his own body, and the stripped skeletal remains of his meal. He thought of the plan he had glimpsed in the creature's mind, and then his thoughts came clearer still. Frank reached into his pocket, pulled out the photo and gazed at it for a long time. A droplet of blood traced a tear's path down his fleshless cheek, but Frank didn't notice. He didn't curse the creature for taking his cab, either; he would be faster on foot, and most of the vehicles in the world would be useless metal clogging up what used to be highways and freeways in a few days. Frank felt his hunger twisting his gut once more, and he threw his head back and howled.

Not far away, a similar sound came back to him. It was spreading.

Frank began to run.

* * *

He was halfway across town when the hunger took him again. Every other thought fell away as his predatory stride gave way to a starving fumbling stumble. A woman watched him spill onto the sidewalk; she approached him with kind words, and an outstretched hand.

Frank ate her, all of her. He couldn't stop, even when he heard people screaming at him or felt them kicking at him. In the midst of the feast he grabbed more than one person, bit them and tossed them aside. He heard cars smashing into one another, and a chorus of screams, but they did nothing to turn him from feasting. By the time she was bones the street was full of mindless rambling monsters. There was no way to tell how many had turned to killing machines but to count the howls he heard from what seemed like every direction.

As his mind came back to him once more, Frank looked around at what he had done. He took the picture from his jacket, as if trying to remind himself of something. His clumsy talons left a streak of blood across the image. Stuffing it back in his pocket, he began to run again. The next block looked normal, other than him loping along the street slightly faster than the vehicles it was made for. It was easy to tear a man's arm off as he passed, to take the edge off while he ran. Frank was a block away before he heard the man scream behind him; another block and he dropped the bony remains of the man's arm in the gutter.

Five minutes later, Frank stood in the street as the sun went down. He nibbled on a head that he had torn off before leaving the business district. There wasn't much meat on the bloody ball, but the skull had split open as he had worried at it with his hunger; the soft warm gooey treat inside was something to be savored. It seemed this might be the most satisfying part of his new diet.

The streetlights came on, startling him and sending him to skulk in the shadows. Even as he backed into the darkness, Frank's rusted eyes stayed fixed on one window. It was on the third floor, bright with light but covered by a curtain. For several minutes that's all he did, stare at the glowing cloth while sucking delicious slime from cracks in the skull in his hands. Then the curtain moved aside, and he dropped the brainless ball to the ground.

Frank stared at her, slack-mouthed. After a moment he spoke, the first word he had uttered with his mangled new voice.

"Maria..." he muttered.

It sounded like gravel on glass, or a monster contemplating a meal; his voice sounded nothing like a man speaking the name of the love of his life. Another bloody tear trickled down Frank's fleshless cheek.

"Hey pal."

Frank started, swung his head to the sound. The voice was like his own, hideous and hungry. The monster standing beside him was as terrifying as he surely looked.

"You going to eat that?" The other monster flashed his rows of teeth in a horrific smile. He glanced at the silhouette of flesh in the window, looked back at Frank. He winked salaciously.

Frank tackled him, and they went down together on the sidewalk. He bit into the monster's arm as it came between them, and spit out the mouthful of sinew immediately. Something in him screamed at him, trying to stop him; the only message he heeded was that this flesh was not food. When a few more bites made the other monster's head loll, and his body go limp, Frank stood and dragged him back into the shadows. He fell on the twitching creature as the light came back into its eyes. The savage swipes of his talons tore it to shreds under him, and his clamping jaws ripped it to so many pieces in the shadows. When Frank's frenzied movements slowed and stilled at last, there was nothing but a slick bony puddle where the monster had lain a minute earlier.

It was impossible for him to resist the cry of hunger building within him. Frank howled at the dark night sky, watching the pane of light on the third floor as the silhouette moved away and the curtain swished shut. A thousand other monstrous voices sounded their own hunger across the city in response. His howl died down as the light in the window winked out, and Frank crept quietly across the street to curl up at the entrance to the building.

* * *

The morning sun felt like a thousand tiny crowbars against the only weak part of Frank's powerful new body. His thin eyelids twitched and contorted on his face until the movement woke him. Frank shielded his eyes with his arm; still the thin translucent scraps of flesh ticced with the regularity of a clock. Moaning, he rolled over on the stair and onto the sidewalk.

Hunger twisted his insides, and Frank came awake completely. He looked down; at his talons, at his torn and bloody clothes, at his long powerful limbs under the painted rags. His belly grumbled and stabbed starving pangs that ate away Frank's thoughts until all that remained was hunger. He took the bloody image out of his pocket, stared blankly at it for a moment, and then put it back. Sniffing the air with the open cavity that used to be his nose, Frank smelled the intoxicating odor of fresh flesh. He also smelled the scent of a flower in bloom, woven delicately into one of the odors. The hunger twisted his guts painfully, and an involuntary growl escaped his lips.

Staggering across the street, Frank saw nothing but heat everywhere he looked. He tripped on the sidewalk, careened off a street sign, and stumbled over a bench before he finally adjusted to his vision enough to not bang into things. The bright morning light had driven his brothers and sisters into hive hiding until nightfall; Frank didn't know how he knew it, but somehow he did. There were a few mindless creatures rambling about on the streets; he could feel them too, sort of. They were sure to leave him alone, though; or offer their flesh to him.

He went as far as he could from home without collapsing from hunger. There was no concern about choosing the wrong block, or heading the wrong direction; he simply needed to be away from home. If someone had stopped and asked him what 'home' meant, Frank could not have formed the thoughts or the words required to answer; he probably would have eaten them before the question could even be asked.

The moment he caught the scent of fresh

flesh, and knew it was not a familiar odor, Frank dropped to all fours. He could hear heartbeats thirty yards away; now twenty; and now, ten. Rounding a corner, Frank approached the three young men loading weapons on a long table in their garage. The wide door stood open, and all three of the men were muscled and shirtless. One had a red bandana tied about his neck.

Frank stood up, looked from one flaming heat signature to another. He howled his hunger, and dropped to all fours again.

One man shot him before his taloned hands hit the drive. The other two had pistols in their hands before Frank could move, and bullets from all three weapons drove him back as he stood once more. He shuddered as they paused together, and a dozen spent rounds were pushed from his flesh to fall at his feet. They sounded like a bicycle bell ringing, or a rolling food cart announcing chow time.

Launching himself forward against the next volley of rounds, Frank took out the table and two of the men in one mighty leap. The three of them went down together in a heap, and their guns clattered to the floor. Turning, the third man knelt to grab a fallen shotgun. He rose to his full height and emptied it into the mess of friends and enemy tangled at his feet. Most of the spraying shots found Frank, and he twitched with each new pattern of red dots that appeared on his face and chest. One of the other men lost his head in the scuffle, part of it blown off by birdshot and the rest bitten off by Frank's furiously chomping rows of teeth.

The other man was stronger than Frank expected, and he kept pulling him down beside him as Frank tried to stand. He felt more like a crab in a bucket than a powerful monster in the midst of a feeding frenzy. The third time his feet came out from under him, Frank saw the man that was still standing dig an automatic rifle from the pile of fallen weapons. Falling on the fallen man, Frank stopped trying to get away and grabbed him. His long talons slipped between the man's ribs, and he gasped in pain as Frank rolled them both over.

Holding the man about the middle, Frank felt the body tremble in his grasp as his friend filled him with bullets. A few went all the way through him, smacking Frank about the face and chest; most stayed in the now lifeless package of flesh hanging from his clawed grip. When the bullets stopped coming, and the body stopped twitching, he cast it aside and stood to tower over the last man standing. The man swung the rifle at his head; Frank batted it aside. The man kicked him in the stomach; Frank howled his hunger at him. The man peed his pants; Frank ate his face.

They went down together, and Frank kept eating. He stripped the corpse clean, then moved to the other two and dug out their brains with his talons. He was sucking the last bit of brains from the third skull when a dirt bike pulled up in the drive. Frank heard the little motor rumble loudly to a stop. He lifted his head and met eyes with the young woman settling the kickstand. She went pale, tried to get the bike going again.

Frank was beside her with one leap; he pulled her from the bike as gently as possible. The young woman smelled more like death than dessert. There were two paper bags in the basket mounted to the seat, and he peered inside. Human food filled both bags, canned goods and crackers and cookies. Frank took one bag from the wire basket and set it next to the woman where she had sprawled in the driveway. She watched him, her eyes wide with terror, as he got on the motorcycle and pushed it forward off the stand. Still not moving, she watched him roll backwards into the street, start the engine, and ride away. She didn't get up and retrieve the bag until the sound of the motor had died completely away.

Walking into the garage, she looked at the mess of blood and bodies on the floor. She closed the open doors on the bullet-riddled old van. She picked up two handguns that were not spent or painted in wet red streaks, and put them in the bag. Then she pressed the button on the wall, and the rolling door began to noisily clatter shut. Picking her way through the corpses, she identified one in particular and took a moment to spit in what was left of his face.

The garage door finished its descent just as she went through the side door and closed it behind her. She locked it, moved the refrigerator against it, tucked the pistols in her waistband, and unpacked the food.

* * *

Frank lined the groceries carefully along the street, from the building's entrance to the motorcycle on the far sidewalk. There were two small boxes that he stuffed absently in his pocket, the one with the bloody picture in it. He skulked in the shadows, and hid from the sun as it rode high and hot in the sky. Watching the window above him, he thought he saw the curtain part at least once. He couldn't be sure. If the door opened, he would hear it; even then, he would stick to the shadows and watch. She couldn't see him, not like this; and how could his son possibly be expected to handle the monster he had become?

A bloody droplet leaked from his eye as he waited. When a bedraggled man came walking up the street, and stopped at a can of food at his feet, Frank leaned forward in his hiding place. A low growl issued involuntarily from his throat.

The man looked around, his eyes going wide and his heart pounding so loud it thrummed in Frank's ears. He bent, picked up the can of peaches, and ran. Frank considered going after the man; the thought of her looking out the window just as he placed a bloody can of peaches back in its spot deterred him. Maybe she had seen that it was safe, or would realize it as the food began to go missing.

It happened several more times, and each time he had to growl to keep the humans from taking more than one item. One brave young man approached the motorcycle, even after Frank had growled at him; he had to stick his head out of the shadows and show the man how many teeth he had before he would finally run away. By the time night began to fall all of the items were gone, except the bike. Frank had chased one of the humans down, but only to slake his gnawing hunger; he didn't put the smashed box of cookies back where it had been.

He heard howls begin to echo throughout the city. The sun wasn't quite down, but early risers were waking to their gnawing need for fresh flesh. Frank felt his own hunger stab at him as steps sounded in the street once more. They stopped, and he peered at the young woman as she stared at the motorcycle. She approached it, looked around, and got on. Frank recognized her by smell more than her youthful features. It was the same overwhelming scent of death that had turned him aside earlier.

Frank let her take the bike; it was hers, after all.

* * *

Frank wished she would stop looking out the window. It was enough that she had a dim light burning; with all their quiet words and careful steps, and the curtain moving aside all too often, they were alerting howlers for blocks. They came one at a time, and he was grateful at least for that. He had already taken out two, and his own hunger was beginning to twist his insides into knots. One more battle, and Frank was afraid that he would have no choice but to feed. Otherwise, he would surely mount the very steps that he guarded, and eat his love and his purpose before his thoughts came back to him.

It was as if the concern took shape before his eyes the moment Frank chose to worry about it. A howler came loping down the street on all fours, swinging his heavy head left and right as he ran. He skidded to a stop in front of the building, lifted the open cavities that used to be his nose and sniffed the air. Frank watched the curtain, willing it to stay closed; again, his worry became reality before his eyes. The curtain moved to the side, and he could clearly make out the darkened silhouette in the dim light. She glowed with heat, with life; and pulsed with the quick hot pumping of blood.

Glancing at the monster at it clacked its teeth and scratched long rivulets in the blacktop, Frank edged closer in the shadows. His feet wanted to run, but past the other monster and up the narrow stairs. His talons wanted to tear, his teeth longed to bite; but not the other monster. It took Frank a long trembling moment to direct his thoughts where he wanted them to go; by the time he had collected himself, the other monster had turned his way.

It growled at him, glanced at the window. It looked like she was watching the monster. As both of their gazes moved from the window, their rusted eyes locked.

"There's plenty in there to go around," the creature said.

Frank realized what the howler meant as an image appeared in his head. The colors and lines were different than when he imagined something, and somehow more clear. For the first time, his attention went to the lower floors; nearly all of the apartments in the building had at least one or two heat signatures in them. The only one he had been able to think about was the one that smelled of fresh blooming flowers; and he could't think about it, not really.

His hunger was too much for Frank to respond. If he let up on the hold he had on himself, he would blur past the other monster and crash through the door.

The creature laughed. It was a horrific

sound, twisted and tortured humanity muddled by rows of sharp teeth and the hundreds of mouthfuls of flesh they had chewed.

"Not in your own backyard, even?" He smiled, and Frank saw the terrifying mirror image of himself in him.

Pulling back further into the shadows, Frank shook his heavy head.

"Go," the howler said. "Feed. I will start on the first floor. I will stop others of our kind from entering the building. Get back here before I get to the third floor."

Frank nodded. He tried to speak, to thank him; the words came out a garbled mess of hungry sounds. He watched the other monster look up at the window again, squinting his eyes to see as only a howler could.

"Save them," he said, quietly. "It's your purpose."

The meaning of the words were lost on Frank. He backed away further, until his retreat was beyond her lofty viewpoint; then he ran, stumbled, and ran some more. Frank didn't even realize he was howling until he heard someone scream nearby. He skidded to a halt, lifted his wrecked face to the wind, and changed course. He howled again.

* * *

It was a simple thing to chase the other howler from the building; Frank sent him an image of the man he had left trapped in his own bathroom. Then he sent an image of two mighty monsters battling over one little building; the creature fled. Frank settled in on the stoop, blocking the battered doorway with his body. He cradled two lifeless heads in the crook of his arm, to slake his hunger when he woke in the morning.

Frank needed a plan; there were more howls than ever sounding throughout the city, and fresh flesh had been much harder to find than the night before. Frank knew what was happening to the people that weren't completely eaten; they were mindlessly roaming the streets, looking to bite someone. Then they would be like him, and so many others hunting by heat. He felt their minds filling the city as surely as he heard their howls filling the night; it wouldn't be long before he was overwhelmed by their hunger, or his own.

He peeled the flesh from the skulls while he thought it over, pausing occasionally to lick blood from bone. By the time the second jaw clattered to the sidewalk, he had a solution. Frank curled his powerful body around what remained of his last two victims' heads and drifted off into a peaceful sated slumber.

* * *

The first stabbing ray of sunlight jolted him awake, and the hunger twisted Frank's guts as he backed into the building. Immediately he smelled blood; blood spilt, and blood pumping. He scrambled forward on all fours, to retrieve the skulls where he had dropped them. Frank had left the eyeballs in them, to keep the gooey superfood inside as fresh as possible; they were watching him dully.

He cracked both skulls over his knee, one in each hand. He ate and licked and sucked at the cracks until the only thing coming from either of them was a high wet whistling sound. Dropping them in the carpeted hallway, he shielded his eyes with one arm and ran as quickly as he could. He didn't look back to see if the curtain moved aside; for her sake, he hoped it didn't. Frank wasn't the only howler out here, skulking in the shadows, learning to hunt when least expected. He had to be quick.

Bursting through the bay window with a powerful half-blind leap, Frank nearly careened off the motorcycle parked in the middle of the living room. He watched the kneeling form of the young woman before her altar. She was rocking back and forth, in a daze, and continued to do so for nearly a minute. He heard her muttering under her breath, about love and purpose. As he approached her, she turned. She stayed on her knees, trembling, watching him.

Frank moved slowly toward her, pulling two small boxes from his pocket in one clumsy handful. The bloody photo drifted to the floor, unnoticed. He held them out, a box in each hand. Desperately, she launched herself at one of the boxes. She tore it open, twisted the cap off the bottle inside, and took two pills. Her eyes rolled back in her head, and she fell unconscious to the floor.

Launching himself through the same hole he had come through, Frank loped to the nearest shopping district and filled a cart with bags of food and water. It took the better part of an hour, and he ran across two looters while he looted. One had hacked at him with a sword; the other had emptied a clip's worth of nine millimeter bullets into his belly; both of their heads were in a styrofoam cooler on top of the bags of groceries and toiletries. Their flesh was in his belly; their blood was in his bones.

He navigated the cart awkwardly through the cluttered streets, back to the young woman's house, shielding his eyes with one hand and pushing with the other. As he rolled it up the drive, the sudden silence of the rattling wheels gave way to another sound. Frank could hear voices inside the house. He listened, creeping up to the broken window quietly.

"Where's the van, Carla?" That was the strongest heartbeat talking, the heat signature that towered over her and spoke in angry tones.

"I left it downtown." Frank had only heard her voice in desperate whispered prayer. It surprised him; strong and defiant as she sounded, her heartbeat was the weakest in the room. Every soft struggled thump sounded like it might be her last. He could hear the way she was controlling her breath; it was still ragged, labored, and thick with fluid.

"Why did you do that?" That was the first voice again; his heartbeat was escalating. Frank bit what was left of his lower lip, to keep from growling or salivating.

"Yeah, Carla, why did you do that?" His heartbeat was racing, but not as strong as the first man's. Probably drugs. Frank frowned; he didn't like drugs.

The third man stayed quiet, and so did his heartbeat. It was strong and steady, as was the hand he was using to point a pistol at her. The other two men were armed, but they were waving their guns around like they were props. The third man was ready to shoot her.

Frank went for him first, and bit off that steady arm in one bite. His hand and the gun fell to the floor. The other two men swung his way and started shooting. More bullets pummeled the man he had just bitten than found Frank, and he howled as the few that did were pushed free of his flesh. The men fumbled with their weapons, trying to insert new clips, as a wet stain formed down the front of one man's jeans. Moaning, overcome with fresh hunger, the rambler stepped past Frank to attack what used to be his friends.

Turning to him, Frank put a taloned hand on his shoulder. He shook his head. The rambler held his remaining arm to Frank's face, an offering; Frank shook his head again. He shoved the monster through the hole in the wall, and howled again; a fresh spray of bullets caught him as he turned, and Frank stumbled backward into the motorcycle. It tipped, and he tumbled to the floor with it. He heard them shouting as he gathered his strength.

"Yeah!" one cried. "Take that, zombie motherfucker!"

"Yeah!" the other echoed. "Yeah, zombie motherfucker!"

Frank lifted the bike off of him with one arm, pushed himself up off the floor with the other. Setting the bike gently back on its stand, he turned to them. He howled. The other man peed his pants as well. Then Frank was upon them, biting and clawing at both of them until there was nothing left but their heads. He wiped his bloody maw on his bloody sleeve, tore their heads off and tossed one through the opening in the wall. He was right, it was drugs; that brain was no good. The flesh, on the other hand, had been adequate.

He turned to the young woman; she still didn't smell like food, and Frank was glad for it. Motioning her to the window, he pointed outside. The cart was still there, although the cooler had been ripped apart. The heads were gone, and so was the rambler he had shoved outside. A woman with a rifle was approaching the cart, cautiously; Frank could see the howler stalking her from the shadows. It was starving, surely the rambler he had tossed outside plus a belly full of brains; he needed to feed better than that to transform completely into a monster as powerful as Frank.

Leaping through the hole, Frank got to the woman at the same time as the other howler. He was blinded by the sudden burst of blood and sunlight, and he clawed at his own eyes until the cart was visible again. The monster was feeding, becoming more of a monster, and Frank let him. He pushed the cart onto the front lawn and started handing her bags and boxes through the hole. Then he tossed the cart into the living room, and piled it and all the furniture he could find against the hole he had made. He crossed the room, pointed at her belly.

She shook her head.

Frank nodded; he didn't dare smile. He knew he was a monster. He moved toward the only unblocked doorway.

"Wait," she said.

He stopped, turned. Frank didn't try to speak; he knew his voice would be horrific, and twisted.

"Is this yours?" she asked. She held out

the photo; Frank noticed that her hand was trembling, her face pale. He nodded.

"Is that your family?" she asked.

Frank nodded again, his eyes filling with bloody tears.

Carla was still holding out the photo. He didn't reach out, so she turned it over and looked at it.

"You have a beautiful family," she said. A streak of red traced its way down one of Frank's fleshless cheeks. "Are they...still alive?"

He nodded, and moved toward the door again.

"I think I'm supposed to help you," the young woman said resolutely. "I think I'm supposed to help you and your family."

Frank shook his head, took another step toward the door.

"Please," she said behind him. "I'm sick. Without doctors, without medicine, I will die. I am okay with that. I am not okay with giving up before that moment comes, however. Please. This is my purpose."

That word threw a switch in Frank, and he nodded. He still didn't trust his voice to make words, to not frighten her; instead he gestured and grunted as politely as possible until she got his meaning. She gathered all the food into packaging that wasn't covered in red wet streaks, and started to pack it into the little basket mounted to the front of her motorcycle. Frank shook his head and pointed at the cart. He grabbed the edges of it and lifted it, to show her that he could carry it if need be. He nodded at the motorcycle, hoping she would remember his earlier display of strength. Carla packed the basket full of food and water, both from his looting and from her cupboards.

When the basket was full, Frank went to the garage and pointed at the scattered weapons. He pointed at the motorcycle again. Carla filled the basket with pistols and ammunition, and a single sawed off shotgun. Then Frank put his hand over his mouth, breathed in and out forcefully into his bent fingers. Carla laughed, went into a room and came out with a clunky plastic and metal device; it had tubes and cords poking from it in nearly every direction. Frank took it from her, gently, and set it in the cart. He pulled a colorful throw from the sofa, tossed it over the cart clumsily. Smiling, Carla moved forward and tucked the blanket in around the load.

"Let's go save your family," she said.

ABOUT CARLA'S PRAYER

I hope you enjoyed 'Frank's Purpose'. It was both the most touching and the most gruesome of the short stories, in my opinion. Titling this volume 'The Heart of the Monster' was a call that was too easy to make. From Frank's dedication to his family to the extreme measures he took in protecting them, that story represented the world of 'Zombie Zero' in a unique way. I was excited to share it with newsletter subscribers first, just as I am excited to be compiling it into book form last.

This next story was another question, brought up by the events that happened in the last one and the one that comes after it. I wrote 'Carla's Prayer' after starting both of them, but again saw that the order didn't work best that way. As much as this story stands on its own, it also serves as a bridge between 'Frank's Purpose' and 'Maria's Hero'. On top of that, it's one of the shortest stories in the collection. It worked out, as all of this somehow did, because the other two stories in this set ran a bit on the long side.

The last thing I wanted to do was end this book on a super short story, and leave you standing on a bridge. That's no way to leave someone wanting more.

We met Carla in that last story, and meeting her was enough to make me want to know more about her. It ended up being a surprise of the most pleasant kind, when I connected more deeply with her. Where I expected to find darkness, I saw light instead. Where I was sure I would encounter hopelessness, I found a toughness like I had never imagined. The decision to write Carla's story quickly showed me that this was another meaningful story, and that it was indeed the perfect bridge between one touching tale and another.

I hope you enjoy reading 'Carla's Prayer' as much as I loved writing it. It was a special thing to connect with her, it's a special thing to connect with you, and it's a sacred thing indeed to be able to connect with you through her. As much as I may tend toward the dramatic in pretty much every aspect of my actual life, there's a special something about quiet strength that makes it a subject of unending interest to me.

But I'm no example of that.

I'll let Carla take that role.

CARLA'S PRAYER

Carla knelt before the colorful altar, her head bowed. The words she murmured were not nearly as important as opening her heart to the Virgin Mother. Carla had gotten through everything else with the Mother's help, bent but unbroken; she would get through this too.

"Please, Mother, help me be patient. Help me be wise."

Prayers were not for games and toys for Carla; she never asked for anything that would get old, or break. She prayed for wisdom, for strength, and for another day of labored breaths. This morning, her prayers were interrupted. Something hit the back of her head, hard; a burst of pain lit up her skull as the object fell jangling to the floor.

"Get moving, girl," a voice said behind her.

Heaving in a breath, Carla turned. She was still kneeling.

"What are you doing awake, Jose?" she asked.

"Getting ready to defend my castle,"

he said, puffing up his chest. He pulled the pistol from his waistband and chambered a round, to make his point. Carla leapt to her feet, then tottered in place while her head swam.

"Put that away," she snapped. "What are you talking about?"

"You went to bed before the news last night." Jose waved the weapon in no particular direction. "There's been some kind of outbreak. The infected are eating people."

Carla laughed. "You and your boys drank too much beer last night, and you watched a zombie movie? That's why you're waving a gun around in my house?"

"My house," he corrected her, letting the wave of the barrel stop when it pointed vaguely at her.

"Put that away," Carla frowned. "Before you shoot something, or break something."

"You go get food," Jose sneered. "I'm in charge of keeping you safe."

Carla shook her head. "By sending me out looting?"

"The boys are coming over," he said. "We'll have the house secured by the time you get back. Make sure you get beer."

He nodded at the keys at her feet, the

jangling object that he had struck her with. Carla shook her head again.

"You want me to take the bike?"

"You have to take the bike," Jose said. "The streets are clogged with abandoned and broken down cars. The van won't stand a chance."

"I'm not getting you beer, then," she said, bending to pick up the keys.

Jose crossed the space between them in one stride; he struck her across the face with the back of his hand as she stood. The blow rocked Carla backward; she dropped the keys.

"If you don't get beer, don't come back," Jose spat.

"I have to use my nebulizer before I go," Carla muttered, bending again to pick up the keys.

"Puff on that thing when you get back," Jose snapped. "We need beer. Get moving, before I start breaking things."

Carla brushed past him, moved to the front door.

"Go through the garage," Jose said. "I already barricaded the front door. You're welcome, by the way. It's probably why you're still alive."

He nudged her as she walked past him

again, and Carla stumbled for a step. She hurried across the tiled floor, let her hand fall on the doorknob.

"Your lip is bleeding," Jose said. "You might want to clean that up."

Carla went through the door, slamming it shut behind her. She left the garage door open when she saw a battered car pull up to the curb. She saw Luis, walking out into the street and waving, but she didn't stop or turn her head. If he saw her lip, it would break her brother's heart; then he would break Jose's teeth, or nose, and she would have to live with that. Instead she made a beeline through a carefully manicured yard to get to the market. Already her breaths were coming shorter, and Carla felt like she was going to throw up every time she hit a bump.

She rolled past the first store she came to; it was a ridiculous mess of broken glass, screaming people and fights breaking out. After motoring around, Carla spotted a corner market that looked unmolested. She took her helmet off and threw it through the plate glass door, praying for forgiveness under her breath as it burst into a million pieces. Carefully, she picked her way through the broken shards and made her way into the building.

Flipping a switch, Carla said a silent thanks as the stocked shelves were bathed in fluorescence. She grabbed four bags from behind the counter, stuffing two with canned goods, crackers and cookies. Two boxes from the pharmacy booth went into one of the first bags. The other two she filled with beer and candy bars, beef jerky and booze. Carrying the heavy bags that she had loaded up for the boys, Carla ducked through the broken remains of the door and stepped into the street. For a moment sunlight blinded her; she blinked it away.

"Hey!" she called out. "That's my bike!"

Two teenaged boys were crouched in the street next to her motorcycle, looking for keys or a way to get around them. One of them stood up, pointing a pistol at her.

"Not anymore," he said.

"Do you even know how to ride it?" she asked. The bags were getting heavy in her arms, and her breaths were coming harder, but Carla tried to keep calm. The boys looked at each other, shook their heads together. She stepped forward, set the bags on the street between them.

"That was the last of what I could find in there," she lied. "Please take it, let me keep my bike."

Each of them grabbed a bag; they ran away hooting. Carla slipped back into the store and retrieved the other two. She wasn't going back for more beer; she needed that bike to get home.

Carla didn't duck back through the doorway quickly enough; a man was approaching her bike, making as if to get on it. Before she could call out, a blur streaked between them. It struck the man, snarling and growling, and took a giant bite out of his arm.

She stared, her eyes wide. It was a cross between a man and a monster, with rows of jagged teeth and long razored talons. Its eyes were wide and rolling and rusted red; there was nothing but hunger in them. It wasn't just biting the man; it was eating him. When it got to a bone it would break it, and suck the marrow from it; when it hit a vein, it would pause to suck it like a straw until the blood stopped pumping or the hunger overtook it again. The man being eaten was embracing the monster for some reason, driving its head further into the wounds as it bit and broke him.

Carla screamed.

The monster stopped feeding, lifted its gaping nostrils to sniff the air. It cocked its head to one side, looking right at her with those red rolling eyes, and went back to feeding on the fallen man. Carla ran to the bike, stuffed the bags in the basket, and turned the motor over. The whole time she watched the monster, waiting for it to come for her; it never even looked up. Carla drove home as quickly as she could get there.

When she pulled up in the driveway, Carla got the sudden sense that something was wrong. As she killed the motor and kicked the stand, another monster leapt from the garage. Its face and talons were covered in blood, and it sniffed the air as the other had done. Brushing her from the motorcycle, the monster looked in the bags. It lifted one from the basket, set it on the paved drive, got on the motorcycle and drove away.

Carla said a silent thanks, collected herself and the groceries, and stepped over the bodies. Careful not to slip in his blood, she leaned over Jose's corpse and spit in what was left of his face. In the kitchen, she unpacked what remained. She swore, then asked forgiveness for it: the boxes from the pharmacy were missing. Her breaths were short labored gasps now; she couldn't put it off any longer. It was impatient torture, but Carla sat and breathed in the thick vapor until she could almost inhale and exhale normally again.

She moved her brother's bent and broken body, then drove the van right over Jose's gutted corpse. It was too much to wind her way through abandoned vehicles once she got to the shopping district, so Carla looked for a drugstore on foot. The sun dipped low in the sky as she searched, and she heard something howl nearby. The sound was immediately answered by a dozen others just like it. Her quest forgotten, Carla ran to where she had left the van; it was up on blocks, the windows broken and the tires all gone.

Every time she heard a howl, she moved away from it. The pistol in her pants wouldn't do her any good against one of those things; it was for people. After awhile she couldn't tell if she was drifting closer to home or further away from it; either way, Carla was not sure she would survive the night. After wandering for what had to be hours, in any direction that would take her away from the hungry howls that seemed to be everywhere, Carla stopped in the middle of the street and stared.

It was her bike. It was parked right there

on the sidewalk, right out in the open. Carla peered closer; her keys were hanging from the ignition.

Lurching across the street, she settled in the seat and thumbed the ignition. The motor turned right over; Carla kicked the stand out from under her and drove away. It wasn't long before she had oriented herself, and found her way home. She rolled the motorcycle into the living room, kicked up its stand in the middle of the carpet, and moved to kneel before the altar.

"Mother," she murmured. "Thank you for saving me. I know it is not for me that I live. I know you saved me for some special purpose. Please don't make it a baby, Mother. I know it's hard for women like me to get pregnant; please let this be the flu, or my broken body acting up again. I don't know if I would have been strong enough to raise a child in yesterday's world; how could I have one in this? The world is broken, Mother. I cannot survive in a world without medicine, without doctors; you know that. Tell me what my purpose is, Mother. Show me what you need me to do. I will not take my own life, what little of it is left. Without medicine I will get very sick, and soon I will die. I can bear that, Mother, if that is my fate;

if not, show me. Tell me what I must do. Let me be your hand, let me do your will..."

Carla knelt in front of the altar all night, mumbling prayers and drifting in and out of sleep. It was the howls that woke her, or the screams that sounded after; they broke the still silence in the city with chilling regularity until the first rays of the sun shone through the piles of furniture against the wide window. Carla had just drifted off, her chin resting on her chest as her breaths came short and shallow. She whispered wordless sounds in her sleep, or semi-conscious state.

With a resounding crash, the bay window shattered inward. The mountain of furniture became a cloud of broken debris, and a monster burst through the cloud. It crossed the living room slowly, holding out an item in each hand. Carla snatched one of them, tore open the box and the bottle inside. She took one pill, then another.

She collapsed to the floor.

ABOUT MARIA'S HERO

Did you like 'Carla's Prayer'? I hope so, I sure had a great time writing it. Jumping back and forth was the best way to write these. A story from 'Monstrous Consequences' was actually the first one I got started on, the one titled 'Michelle's Luck'. Before I got back to that one, I had finished this set and one other. Although I started 'Carla's Prayer' fourth, I finished it first. I had already started 'Maria's Hero', after beginning 'Frank's Purpose'. Frank's story got wrapped up second, and this one third. It might sound like they went in a nice clean order, and they did in a way; but jumping back and forth was key, for me.

There is a tie-in to 'Zombie Zero: The First Zombie' in this story; you'll find it in the italicized section in the beginning of Chapter Seventeen. It's really more a glimpse of what's happening after this story, deposited at its proper place in the timeline. Of course, these stories all stand alone and together at the same time...so feel free to live in the moment, and get the most of it.

You know, like Carla would.

Quiet faith is as appealing to me as quiet strength. There is plenty of speculation about what lies beyond our world in all of my books, although they lean more towards the deeper meaning in their true higher calling. Life right here right now is where that meaning has the most use, in my experience; and there are so many layers to everything that such exploration never strikes a rock bottom or glass ceiling. I've seen more brands of faith in my life than I have brands of shoes, and I have found that they have the same common problem: they just don't fit me right.

It is the people who spend time in silence that I love to coax into talking about their faith. No matter their spiritual or religious background, that regular time set aside cements something within folks that always seems to show. We all find something different in the stillness, but any road we take brings us to a sacred common ground.

That's where I found Carla, and it was a special thing to start a story with a character on their knees. Peeking into those thoughts made me glad I did, as I saw her asking for work instead of assigning it. It struck me as totally appropriate to end this set and this series with 'Maria's Hero'. I hope you love it!

MARIA'S HERO

Maria pushed aside the curtain, looked out the window. She hoped against all hope that she would see a yellow vehicle searching for a parking spot three floors down; when she saw nothing but white and beige cars drifting slowly down the lane, she let the curtain fall into place again. Maria tried not to feel impatient; she relied on Frank for so much. He was always home as soon as he dropped off his last fare, not off to a bar or a brothel like so many other men. It was unfair for her to wish that there was no final fare at the airport every day, no extra fistful of bills for him to shove at her happily.

It was too much for her to tell him that every time he came home at the end of the day, she felt a crushing weight lift from her narrow shoulders. It was too much to tell him that the money was nothing compared to his arms around her; they needed it, and he worked so hard for it. It was too much to tell him that without him there to cheer her on, Maria trembled and quaked through her days. Raising Juan had been a terrifying prospect; then the doctors had said that he was special, and danced around the meaning of 'special' until Maria had lost her composure. She had cried out in the waiting room, surrounded by frightened or grieving onlookers.

"What is wrong with my son?" she had screamed, to the horror of the evasive doctor and pretty much everyone else in the room. Frank had taken her hand. When the doctor told her to calm down, Frank had spoken to him in the same mellow cadence the physician had been using.

"How can you not see how hard you are making this on us?" Frank had asked quietly. "Are you getting your pleasure from not telling us what you know, or from watching us get more upset as you continue to say nothing? We are parents. We knew that things would have to change when we brought our baby home. Now we see that things need to change even more. We came here to find out what is affecting our son, and how we can deal with it. We do not know how until you tell us what you know. We don't need assurances from a stranger obviously untrained in being assuring. We need to know the diagnosis."

"Your son has a severe case of autism,"

the doctor had said. "There is no cure or known treatment. There are, however, a lot of resources-"

"Thank you, Doctor," Frank had cut him off. "Can we take our son home now?"

Some people have a favorite song or novella or scene that they like to go back to, in their minds or on a lighted screen. The visit fulfills different needs for different people. That was Maria's favorite moment, and she went back to it in her mind at least once every day. That was the day her husband had gone from lover to legend for her, the day the man she loved became a mythic figure in her mind. Frank was her sail, the only reason she had ever had to move in any decisive direction; since then, that moment had been the wind in her sail. There was nothing in her present that past moment couldn't get her through, and there was nothing her hero could do that would knock him from that lofty pedestal.

Letting the covering fall across the window, Maria turned her eyes to Juan. He was curled up on the couch, thoroughly engrossed in the lighted screen in his lap. Every few moments he would swipe a finger from right to left across the screen, and a new page of text would appear. It was difficult to tell if he was in a state of hypersensitivity, keenly aware of her breath and her movements and perhaps even her thoughts; or if he was lost inside himself, unable to hear her voice if it shouted in his ear. It never seemed to be anything in between.

Maria took a deep breath, turned her thoughts to her heart as she watched him read. She felt the tide of love rise within her, felt a smile begin on her face as her spirit lifted. It was a trick she wished she could teach to every parent, putting herself in a place of love and appreciation before speaking to him. Maria got instant feedback from the practice, and had learned it from necessity. If she was frustrated or impatient or melancholy, Juan picked up on it. He might scream at her, or refuse to do as he was asked, or ignore her completely. At first Maria had allowed her frustration to build, which sent Juan deeper into mental seclusion or into a more frantic fit; then she had put herself in his shoes, and wondered what she might do differently.

It didn't always work; but the number of times he responded had switched places with the number of times he didn't immediately. Now it was rare for either of them to get frustrated with the other. When she went out, Maria found herself wanting to lecture parents speaking sternly or absently to their children. She wanted to point out to parents of teenagers that they shouldn't expect their kids to listen to them; they've spent years learning not to, for their own emotional survival. Instead she pushed those thoughts from her mind when she had them, and filled her heart with love and gratitude like Juan had taught her to.

"Sweetie," she said softly. Maria could hear the smile in her voice, and could feel the happy in her heart. "Daddy will be home soon."

Juan swiped to a new page. He kept his eyes on the screen, his body curled into itself.

"Airport fare," he said woodenly. "You don't know when."

Maria smiled. "That's right, Juan. He would have been home by now if he hadn't picked someone up at the airport. Still, I'm sure he'll be here soon. We should be ready, don't you think?"

Juan swiped left. "I'm ready."

"Okay, sweetie," Maria nodded. "I just thought you might want to stick to your reading schedule, or you might need to use the washroom."

Juan's face scrunched in frustration, and

his body curled into an even tighter ball. His eyes drifted to her feet.

"Maybe," he said.

Maria watched him quietly, smiling. She did not suspect or accuse other parents of loving their children less than her; she did know that there was not a parent alive who loved their child more than her. Juan had taught her to deal with her own difficulties as she had watched him deal with his. She had gone from an effusive self-absorbed young woman to a quietly confident mother under his unbending tutelage.

The first few years she had muttered all of her thoughts under her breath as she tended to him and the housework. One day he had repeated them all back to her, the longest string of words he had ever spoken. Maria had been shocked at her own thoughts, and carelessness, and had momentarily envied his inability to connect. That had led to another spiral of guilt, but this time she had kept it to herself; still Juan had remained tense, and more distant than usual. It wasn't until Maria had calmed herself, and gotten ahold of her inner dialogue, that he had relaxed.

After that, Maria behaved as though he could read her thoughts as clearly as the words on his electronic device. She had learned not to be surprised when that seemed to often be the case, as surely as she had learned that she was the one in charge of what thoughts she entertained. Maria had learned so many things from him; the greatest lesson was patience, and it was a lesson than never ended. It might be a minute, or five, while she waited for him to engage again. Patience had taught her to wait; to wait, and think good thoughts.

"Seven minutes," Juan murmured finally. "Seven more minutes."

His head moved to the right, and he glared intently at a patch of carpet that looked like every other patch of carpet on the floor. Maria filled in the rest. The 'please' was in the request itself, and the 'thank you' would possibly never be something to expect. Another parent with another child might have been able to demand eye contact, and probably get it; Maria was so touched by his refusal to view the screen again until she consented, her eyes filled with tears.

"Okay, sweetie," she smiled. "You don't need to use the washroom?"

His face scrunched up again, and he glanced at her feet.

"Seven minutes," he repeated. "Seven minutes."

"Okay, then," she cooed. "Seven minutes."

Juan's face relaxed, and his eyes went back to the lighted screen. A moment later, he swiped left.

Maria went back to the window, pulled aside the curtain. There was a parking spot open right in front of the building; she hoped Frank got home in time to take it. On the coffee table between Juan and Maria, her wireless device chirped insistently.

Juan sat up suddenly, the electronic reader sliding from his lap to the cushion beside him. His whole body was rigid and tense, and his voice was a thin wail as he spoke a single word three times.

"Alert!" he cried. "Alert! Alert!"

"It's okay, sweetie," Maria cooed. "That's probably just Daddy, asking if we want him to bring home anything."

She approached the device, picked it up, lifted it to her eyes. The light was fading. Maria pressed the button at the bottom of the screen. The red banner read 'ALERT: A possible outbreak has occurred in your city. All civilians are advised to remain indoors. Do not to allow anyone entrance to your homes. Wait for further updates."

"Alert!" Juan cried again. "Alert! Alert!"

Maria went to the window, moved the

curtain aside, and looked down at the street below. Frowning, she let the fabric fall back into place.

* * *

"Daddy's here! Daddy's here!" Juan leapt to his feet.

"Stay away from the windows please." Maria's voice was too tense, too strained; the 'please' meant nothing to Juan if it didn't sound pleasing.

Maria took a deep breath, did her best to smile.

"Juan," she said slowly. "The alerts said we should stay away from the windows. Remember? They said it was an emergency situation. You know all about emergency situations. You know what we do in emergency situations."

That stopped him. Juan stood stiff and still a few steps short of the curtain. He gazed intently at the floor. His breathing was loud, hurried.

"Stay calm in an emergency," he muttered. "Let people help in an emergency."

Maria laughed. "That's right. See, you remember better than Mama. Mama forgot to stay calm."

"Stay calm in an emergency," he said again, louder. "Let people help in an emergency."

"That's right," she repeated, quietly. "Do you remember what else the helpful people said? Stay away from windows and what else? Can you help me remember, sweetie? You're so good at remembering things."

"Be quiet!" he cried, excited to recall the information. Juan bit his lip, shook his head quickly. He turned toward Maria, stared at her feet.

"Be quiet," he whispered. "Be quiet, stay away from the windows, don't let strangers in, turn off the lights when it gets dark."

Juan shuffled to the sofa and sat down. His feet were flat on the floor, his knees and waist bent at right angles, his back rigid and straight. He stared at the blank widescreen television.

"Daddy's here," he whispered. "Daddy's here."

"Why do you keep saying that, sweetie?" Maria asked, forgetting herself for a moment.

"Daddy's here," Juan whispered. "Daddy's here."

Maria went to the window. Before she reached out, she turned her whole body to face him.

"Juan," she said. "Mama is going to look out the window to see if Daddy's car is out there. It's okay for me to break this rule, just for this one occasion. Does that make sense?"

"Daddy's here." Juan nodded. "Daddy's here."

Maria turned and reached out, moved the fabric aside. She stepped up to the transparent pane. The spot was still empty, and now the street was too. It was darker than she had thought it would be, and the streetlamp under the window had already flickered on. Pressing closer to the glass, Maria thought she saw movement in the shadows along the narrow lighted lane. She peered into the darkness, pulling back suddenly when she saw a blurred streak dash into the same dark spot she had been watching. Slowly coming closer to the window again, she saw what looked like one animal devouring another on the sidewalk for a split second. Then one of the creatures dragged the other's limp and lifeless body back into the shadows.

Her eyes went round as she watched a tendril of flowing blood exit the shadows, cross the sidewalk, and dribble into the street. The flow grew, the tendril widened, and a puddle began to form on the blacktop.

"Daddy's here," Juan whispered behind her. Maria started.

"Daddy's here," he said again, even more quietly.

A hideous sound filled the air, a monster howling its hunger in the lane below. It wasn't the first they had heard, but it was the closest. It was followed by a dozen others, that she could hear; screams that sounded half animal, half human, and completely terrifying.

Maria let the curtain fall closed. She moved hurriedly about the room, shutting off all but one dim light.

"Do you want to wait for Daddy to get home to eat dinner?" she asked, sitting on the other end of the sofa.

His response was barely a movement; for anyone else, it may have meant nothing. Maria saw his chin move, while his eyes stayed locked in place. It was as obvious as anyone else shaking their head to her. When he nodded, it was much the same; a slight movement that spoke volumes. She didn't know how his actions looked from inside his head; through her eyes they were always either extraordinarily subtle, or incredibly dramatic. The world in between was for everyone else.

"Daddy's here," Juan said after the minuscule movement. "Daddy's here."

*   *   *

"Daddy's gone."

Maria sat up, her eyes going wide. Juan sat at the other end of the sofa rocking back and forth and shaking his head tragically. Maria had a sweet moment to remember waking up for a moment the night before. She had fallen asleep on the couch, waiting past everyone's bedtime for her hero to come sweeping through the door. At some point Juan had curled up beside her while she slept, pressing himself against her in a sublimely shocking show of openness. Maria had come awake, felt him breathing close to her, so relaxed and peaceful. Thankfully, she had drifted off again before she could remember why they were on the sofa together.

"Daddy's gone." Her moment was over. "Daddy's gone."

"Okay, sweetheart," she said. "That's okay. Do you want some breakfast? We should probably eat..."

Maria didn't finish her thought. While we still can? Before the food starts to go bad, or run out? Before a monster tears through the door and eats us both? She breathed, trying to calm herself.

"We should probably eat something," she said.

"Daddy needs to eat," Juan said. He stopped rocking back and forth; the realization had jolted him from his trance. He stared in the general direction of the closed curtain, as if he was trying to look directly at it. He growled low frustration under his breath, then started rocking again. He shook his head violently.

"Daddy needs to eat," he said, bobbing in place. "Daddy needs to eat."

"We need to eat too, sweetie," Maria reminded him gently.

"Daddy needs to eat!"

"Okay, Juan." Maria sighed. "I'm not very hungry anyway. We'll wait for awhile. Not too long, though, okay? You know how cranky Mama gets when she gets hungry."

"Mama needs to eat," he said, smiling the faintest touch of a smile. "Mama needs to stay calm."

"We'll both eat in a little while, okay?" Maria smiled, put her hand on her chest. She didn't know what it was like, for other parents; she did know that the most subtle movement or gesture from her son that acknowledged her was water in the desert to her soul. Maria let her heart fill with its sustenance as tears filled her eyes.

"Stay calm in an emergency!" he cried. Maria laughed, and wiped away her tears.

"Do you want to read, honey?" she asked.

"'Going Green!'" he shouted, startling himself. His voice dropped to a whisper. "Christina McMullen: seasteader, scientist, author. Zombies!"

"I don't know what you're talking about, sweetie."

"'Going Green!'" he whispered fiercely. "Zombie apocalypse. Not walkers; walkers help people deal with their demons. Zombies!"

"Juan," Maria said, quietly. "Would you please stop saying that word?"

She had flipped on the television set, to listen to the constant alerts and learn as much as she could. More than one reporter had used that word, in a completely serious tone of voice. At first she had laughed, uneasily; then Juan had started saying it, and she had tried to explain that the reports must be wrong. She had shown him an episode of the popular television show she had been watching with Frank, and Juan had started screaming "Not walkers! Walkers help people deal with their demons!" every time someone referred to a dead character. Maria had shut off the lighted screen, and hadn't turned it on since. She had given up trying to explain what she herself did not understand.

Sliding the reader closer to him on the coffee table, Maria waited for him to notice it. They sat together, both of them still and silent, until he moved. Standing, he cast his eyes sideways at the curtain. He walked to the dining nook, pulled out a chair, and sat down.

"Daddy's here," he murmured quietly.

Maria walked to the window and moved the fabric aside. She glanced down at the street, felt her eyes widen.

There was a creature in the street, lining cans and boxes of food from the entrance of their building to the other side of the paved lane. A motorcycle was parked on the sidewalk, across the street, and it looked like the creature was making a trail to it from their door. She let the curtain fall back into place, and took a moment to let the color come back into her face before she turned.

The image was so etched into her mind that Maria burned breakfast. Juan was too distant to notice, or too kind to say anything. They ate together in silence, her trying to keep that awful word that everyone kept saying from leaping to mind. She wished she hadn't seen that thing, or the horrible obvious trap it was laying. What should have tasted like burnt bacon and overly refried beans in her mouth was more like flavorless cardboard, and Maria ate only to fill her belly. Every time Juan spoke she would jump a little, and every time he said the same thing.

"Daddy's here," he would say. Sometimes it was a soothing whisper; other times it was a frantic cry. Every time it startled her, and after awhile it frightened her as much as that word she wasn't thinking about. She didn't shush him, or stop eating. Maria kept her breathing calm and even, and her thoughts as bright as she could. When they were finished eating she went to the window and swept aside the curtain. She saw someone on the street, bending to pick up a can of something. She watched him start, then stare into the bushes nearby, then dash off. He took the food, and it looked as though he got away.

Maria sighed, let the curtain fall back into place. She glanced at Juan, already reading on the couch. The difference between their worlds was a subject she considered often, though not nearly so often as it was shoved politely in her face. At ten years old, he had read more books than Maria knew existed; certainly more than she could ever hope to read herself. When she was ten, Maria had been a social butterfly; she had spent her childhood and early adulthood collecting friends like her son now collected books. After falling in love with Frank, her social life had dwindled as she focused on him. When Juan came, Maria let the number of close people in her life come to match her son's number slowly over time. At some point her social life had died altogether, and she hadn't even noticed.

It wasn't for her that she pondered their differences, except in her selfish desire to see her son happy. Maria watched every day for another line to stretch out between their worlds. It had started with books; they never taught him to read, but he had been obsessed with their old library from the time he could crawl. Frank had read westerns as a boy, and she had read her share of teenage romance novels. Neither of them had thought anything of it when he would walk around with one of them, or leaf through its pages. They both assumed any ability he would ever have to read would be developed over time, slowly, like the other simple skills they had so much trouble teaching him.

His first long sentence had befuddled them both. Juan had approached them on the couch one day, looked at his mother's feet, and announced, "Anne is in love with Todd but Raina doesn't know it."

Frank had started laughing. "He thinks one of your daytime novellas is real," he had said.

Maria had shaken her head. "Anne is the name of one girl, but there's no Raina. There's definitely no Todd. Those are North American names."

She had nudged him, playfully, and added, "Also, I only watch one novella. I spend the rest of my day taking care of our house and our son."

"And a wonderful job you do of it," he had replied, kissing her cheek. "So what is he talking about?"

"I think..." Maria had paused, smiled, changed her tone of voice. "Juan, sweetie, can I see the book you're carrying?"

Juan's eyes had gone wide. His gaze had shifted to his father's shoes, as they often did when he wanted Frank to override her.

"Just for a minute," Maria had assured him.

"Mama said just for a minute," Frank had spoken soothingly.

"One minute," Juan had held out the book, still glaring at his father's shoes. As soon as her hand had touched it, he'd spoken again. "Sixty."

Maria had taken the book, glanced at Frank. "Did you teach him numbers?"

"Fifty-nine," Juan had said, a little louder.

Frank had shaken his head, his eyes going round with wonder.

"Fifty-eight," Juan had gotten just a little louder, again.

Maria opened the book on her lap, leafed through the pages while he counted down. He didn't miss any numbers, and his voice continued to rise in volume as he spoke them. By the time he got to twenty he was nearly shouting, and Maria had pointed out the names he had spoken throughout the book a half dozen times to Frank. She had also pointed out a couple of scenes that had been a bit much for her at fourteen. Flushing, she had handed the book back to her son.

Juan had fallen silent, his face red from exertion. Maria and Frank had exchanged a bewildered look, then Frank had looked up at Juan.

"Do you know the other numbers, son?"

he had asked. "Can you count up from one to where you left off?"

"Onetwothreefourfivesixseveneight-nineteneleventwelvethirteenfourteenfif-teensixteenseventeeneighteennineteen..."

Juan had stopped, after saying them all in one breath and all as one word. He had sat next to his father on the sofa, with a clear space between them, opened the book and started reading.

"Our three year old son can read," Frank had whispered to her, his voice touched with awe.

"And he can count," Maria had murmured, kissing his cheek.

"Also, we apparently don't need to teach him about sex," he'd chuckled.

Maria had flushed again, and they had gone out shopping for more age-appropriate reading material. Juan showed no interest in pictures or children's books; so they had beefed up their library, to see him light up every time a new book was placed in his hands. It had gotten expensive very quickly, and Maria had suggested that they give ebooks a try. After the initial investment in the device, Juan's voracious appetite for reading was finally something they could satisfy while staying within their budget.

It had been a long thin cord stretched out between their world and his, and they had strengthened the connection in every way they could.

Her life was dedicated to stretching as many of those connecting cords between their worlds as possible. Maria knew she couldn't expect to build a bridge, to see her son walk into her world; she knew she would never walk into his. Still she lived to see the two grow more connected; every time he lit up, she walked on clouds all day. She thought about the differences between them until the curtained window grew dark and howls began to sound in the city. Every once in a while she went to the window, until all of the food in the street had disappeared. She watched a young woman ride away on the motorcycle as the streetlights came on.

Just when it was most important for her to stay away from the window, Maria felt drawn to it like a metal filing to a magnet. It kept getting darker, and she kept going to the window. Her eyes would go from the blood in the street to the shadows behind it, then back to the blood. The light of the streetlamp gave the dried puddle an orangish hue, and the shadows revealed none of its dark secrets to her.

She saw a monster approaching the building, one of the times she looked out. Maria had pressed herself closer to the window, unable to look away as it casually crossed the street. The shadow she had been watching had come alive behind the creature, and another monster had burst forth to tackle the one approaching the building. They had battled in the street, but only for a few moments; the element of surprise gave the attacking monster an extra fatal second. It was all the creature needed to tear the other to pieces under the streetlight; as Maria watched, the victor dragged the loser into the shadows.

Now she had two puddles of blood to watch, and one frightful shadow. Maria was grateful to see Juan wrapped up in reading; she couldn't seem to calm herself. When she saw another creature torn to bits in the street, her hands started to tremble. She sat at the far end of the sofa, trying to fill her whirling mind with happy images. Every sunny picnic she imagined was torn apart by monsters; every sweet memory she pictured was ripped to shreds by zombies. Maria sat still, resisting the urge to go to the window, until Juan sat up and spoke.

"Daddy needs help," he whispered

intensely. He stared at the dark television screen as if it was lit by an engrossing scene. He spoke again, with the soft supplicating tone of voice he only used when addressing his father.

"Let people help in an emergency," he murmured. "Let people help in an emergency."

Juan began to rock back and forth, his eyes locked on the blank screen. Her resolution forgotten, Maria went to the window. She brushed the curtain aside, looked down from her vantage point. A monster was standing there, in the middle of the street. It was looking up at her. Maria felt icy prickles climb her spine, but she couldn't look away. She watched as the monster turned its back on her, stared into the shadows behind it. She wondered if the other creature was still hiding in the foliage, if they were maybe having a nice little monster chat. Still she watched, until the creature in the street turned in his tracks and began walking toward their building. Finally she let the curtain fall back into place, and went to sit on the sofa once more.

The explosion of wood and glass when the creature went through the door pulled a surprised shriek from Maria's lips. She glanced over at Juan; he was reading, either unaware of the situation or unconcerned by it. She watched him when the first scream sounded; he read seven pages before the next shrill cry filled the air. Juan continued to read, his features relaxed and his breathing calm. Maria found herself wishing that she knew as little or as much as he did, to sit there so sublime. Then she chided herself for her foolishness, and went looking about for a weapon.

Of course there were no guns in the house. Juan might not be able to tie his own shoes without coaching and moral support; but who knew what hidden abilities he possessed? If they bought a safe, could he crack it in his sleep? Would the mechanisms of the weapon inside be a language he knew intimately, or a curiosity he couldn't comprehend? Either way, it was not a chance worth taking. After only a few minutes of searching, Maria sat on the couch again. There was a kitchen knife tucked into her apron, and she held a baseball bat upright between her knees. As one scream after another sounded below them, she gripped the handle of the bat and tried to breathe as calmly as possible.

After what seemed like an eternity, and a very long look at what felt like cowardice and fear to her, the sounds of tortured cries and tumbling bodies below stopped suddenly. Juan looked up from his reader.

"Daddy's here," he said. A slight smile touched the corners of his lips, and it was all she could do to keep from breaking down. Maria trembled, her hands on the sweaty grip of the wooden weapon, watching him. Juan set the device carefully on the coffee table and moved to the dining table. He pulled out a chair, sat down and stared peacefully at nothing. After a few moments he spoke again, his eyes still locked in place.

"Mama needs to eat," he announced. "Mama needs to stay calm."

Maria couldn't hold it in any longer; but rather than burst into tears, she set aside the bat and let them stream down her face while she prepared dinner. She made enough for Frank too, not thinking; somehow she was able to lose herself in putting together the meal. It turned out perfect, and would have been the cause for much exclamation had her husband been there to partake. Frank had always been very vocal about appreciating even her most simple meals; without him there to point it out, Maria couldn't taste it. As far as she knew, Juan never did.

The violent noises below them had not

started up again all night, although more and more howls sounded in the neighborhood. They slept together on the sofa again, and Maria spent a long time just feeling him close before drifting off. She thought back over her life instead of forward to their uncertain future, and counted her blessing in the smiles she had brought to her family's faces. When she slept she dreamed of hope, and not the hungry howls that filled the night.

* * *

In her dream Maria walked into another world; it was a world without zombies, or a missing husband. It was a world where Juan looked her in the eyes, and smiled at her in a way that was neither subtle nor exaggerated. It wasn't for her that she wished a different experience on him, or dreamed of it; it was for him, to see his eyes clear of torment and his features free of fear. There was no guilt in the dream, and she stayed with it longer than she might have normally. When she woke and saw Juan reading peacefully at her feet, Maria let herself drift back into the pleasant alternate reality. She hadn't slept well the night before, and that other world fortified her soul.

A quiet rapping at the door roused her, and for a sleepy moment Maria fretted about her and Juan still being in their pajamas. Then she came to her senses, stood and wrapped her robe about her body. Another knock sounded, a little louder, and Juan moved to stand. Maria put her hand on his shoulder, gently.

"Mama's got it," she whispered.

Juan twisted his body away from the contact, went back to reading. Cinching the belt of her robe about her waist, Maria slid the kitchen knife into the knot. She picked up the bat, moved slowly toward the door. Up on her tiptoes, she could see out into the hallway through the peephole. The moment she placed her eye to it, the woman knocked again. Maria started, moved away from the door. Her heart was pounding in her ears.

"Stay calm in an emergency," Juan murmured. "Let people help in an emergency."

"Shhh, sweetie," Maria whispered.

"I can hear you in there," a woman's voice called out. The knock came again, louder this time. "Please open up. I'm here to help."

Maria bit her lip. "Who are you?"

"My name is Carla." The voice came closer to the door, and she spoke more quietly. "I know you have no reason to trust me, but I swear I am only here to help. Please open up. I'm alone, and I have food for you and your son. I want to help you."

"What do you know about me and my son?" Maria backed away from the door. "Who sent you?"

"Daddy sent her," Juan said behind her. Maria jumped, and whirled to him. Icy fingers climbed her spine. Juan was still reading, oblivious to her alarmed state.

"Stay calm in an emergency," he said, swiping to the left. "Let people help in an emergency."

"What did you say, sweetie?" Maria breathed.

"Stay calm in an emergency," he repeated, still not looking up. "Let people help in an emergency."

"No, sweetie," she said. "Before that."

Juan remained silent, and swiped his finger across the screen.

"Ma'am," the woman's voice came through the door again. It sounded like she was leaning against it. "I would swear on my mother's grave if she hadn't been a worthless waste of a woman. If it means anything to you, I swear on the Virgin Mother that I would never do anything to hurt you or your little boy. On what little is left of my life, I swear that I am only here to help."

Maria sighed, crossed herself and moved to unlock the door. She stood back as it swung inward, clutching the bat before her defensively. When her eyes fell on the young woman, she saw details she hadn't seen through the peephole. There was blood on her clothes, two pistols tucked in her waistband, and a bag of groceries on the floor at her feet.

Dropping the bat, Maria heard it clatter to the floor as she opened her arms to the woman. Carla hesitated, looking down at her bloodstained clothes; then she embraced her, hugging her so hard and so close that Maria felt the butt of one of the guns poking her in the belly. She didn't let go until Carla relaxed; as she stepped back, Carla dug one of the pistols from her waistband. She reversed it in her hand, held the handle out to Maria.

Maria shook her head, stepped past the young woman to look up and down the hallway, then bent to pick up the groceries. She ushered her inside, closed the door behind her and bolted it. As she turned again, she saw Carla preparing to kneel before Juan.

"Oh, no," Maria said. "He doesn't like-"

"Hey little man," Carla said, dropping to her knees. "What's your name?"

Juan set the reader aside, looked at the woman's shirt.

"You're sick," he said, and nodded firmly. "I'm sick too."

"I'm so sorry," Maria blurted, abashed. "He doesn't-"

"He's right," Carla shrugged, glancing up at her. She reached her hand out to him; Maria shook her head in wonder as Juan grasped it, held it tight.

"Daddy sent you," he breathed, pulling her hand to his chest possessively. "To save Mama, and Juan."

Maria bit her lip, watching them together. She saw Carla glance up at her, and cross herself reflexively with her free hand.

"You're right, Juan," Carla smiled. "I prayed to the Mother, and our Daddy in heaven sent me to you. You are the answer to my prayer."

Juan nodded the whole time she spoke, and Maria breathed a little easier. If such darkness as had descended upon the world were possible, why couldn't there be a ray of light? Why couldn't she believe in the unbelievable, when she had already watched it outside her window? Maria signed her own cross across her chest, out of habit.

"Can I talk to your mom for a minute, Juan?" Carla murmured.

He let her hand go, turned and picked up his reader.

Carla exchanged a smile with Maria.

"Your son is amazing," Carla breathed.

Maria nodded. "You're right," she said. It wasn't a statement of pride; it was not a proclamation of her son's greatness, or her own. Maria's simple answer was full of awe for the other woman; she had seen in a moment what it had taken Maria years to realize: maybe 'special' means something more, not something less.

"We need to get you out of here," Carla said firmly.

Maria glanced at Juan. She shook her head.

"Where are we supposed to go?" she asked.

"To the marina," Carla said. "You need to get away from the city, away from the land. We'll find a boat, and load it with supplies."

"And then what?" Maria cried.

"And then you survive," Carla said, thrusting the butt of a pistol at Maria once again. She threw a meaningful glance in Juan's direction. "So does your son."

Maria took the weapon, held it uncertainly in her hand.

"What about you?" she asked.

Carla smiled; it was beautiful, unabashed and open. It took Maria a moment before the words that went with it sunk in for her.

"Oh, I'm dead either way."

* * *

They hadn't gone a block before they saw their first rambler. It was roaming the street, stumbling over its own hunger and moaning mindlessly. Carla stopped in her tracks, pointed at it.

"Ready for target practice?" she nudged Maria playfully.

"Oh, no." Maria shook her head. "I could never shoot someone."

"That's not someone," Carla said, not unkindly. "That is a monster that wants to eat your son."

Maria frowned, looked at Juan. He was holding hands with Carla, at his insistence; it was the only way they could get him to keep moving. She fingered the butt of the pistol she was carrying, frowned. The monster turned, sensing her thoughts or smelling her flesh; slowly it began to shuffle towards them. It moaned as it moved, its eyes rolling maniacally. Every few steps, its head would twitch and bob quickly, the only rapid movement it seemed capable of. Slowly, inexorably, it closed the gap between them.

Glancing at the young woman, Maria brought the pistol up with both hands. Carla opened her mouth to speak as Maria yanked the trigger.

"Hold the handle ti-"

The sound it made was much more than she had expected; the lurch in her hands nearly tore the gun from Maria's grasp. She cried out, her ears ringing; she switched the weapon between hands to shake the pain from them one at a time. She noticed that a car window had burst to pieces far to the right of the ambling creature; it kept trudging toward them, oblivious to the sound and the broken glass.

Carla was talking; all Maria could hear was that dull distant ringing in her ears.

"What?" she shouted.

Smiling, Carla knelt next to Juan. She said something to him; Maria couldn't hear anything but that ringing, and the next words Carla called into her ear as she disengaged from him and stood beside her.

"Hold the handle tight, like this," she cried, moving Maria's fingers so they curled more effectively around the butt of the weapon. "Squeeze the trigger, gently, and keep the single sight at the end of the barrel between the two sights closest to you. Watch and make sure it doesn't drift when you-"

The next shot took them both by surprise. Maria turned to her, eyes wide. "All I did was squeeze!"

Carla nodded, shaking her head to clear it. She smiled.

"That's all you have to do!" she shouted back. "Unfortunately, you also shot another window out of the same car. Is that what you're aiming at? Because you should probably shoot the zombie instead."

Maria shot her a dirty look, playfully, crinkling her nose at the word; she lifted the pistol again.

"Relax," Carla said. "Take your time. Breathe, then hold as you exhale. And boom."

The word was drowned out by the sound, and the rambler's shoulder exploded. It staggered backwards a few steps, twitched convulsively for a disturbing moment, then began walking toward them once more.

"Carla," Maria said, lowering her weapon. "Would you please...?"

In one fluid motion, Carla pulled the pistol from her waistband, aimed and fired; there was no hesitancy, no careful steadying of her hand or breath. The monster's head exploded, and its body crumpled lifeless to the pavement. After, she dropped to one knee. For a moment Maria thought she was praying, or asking forgiveness; as her hearing came back to her, she heard the young woman's labored shallow breathing. Maria dropped to one knee beside her.

"Are you all right?" Maria asked. She put a hand on Carla's shoulder. "Is there anything I can do? Tell me what I can do."

One of her hands was supporting her weight, fingers splayed on the street. Carla waved the other in the air dismissively.

"...am...fine..." she gasped. "...need...a minute..."

Maria did the only thing she could think to do: she prayed. With one hand on Carla's shoulder, and the other over her heart, she prayed like she hadn't in years. A part of her had felt snubbed by God, or at least forgotten, in the frustrating string of moments turned years that she had cried out for guidance or a miracle. It had taken this mysterious young woman to remind her of what she already knew: Juan was a miracle in and of himself; there was no greater gift that could have showered down on her than the constant growth that was sharing his life.

As she prayed, she felt a hand on her shoulder. Maria opened her eyes, and saw Juan standing between them. He had a hand on each of their shoulders, and his head was bowed. She couldn't say for sure that he was praying with her, but that certainly appeared to be the case. When Carla opened her eyes and looked from one of them to the other, they were bright and full of tears. She crossed herself, wiped her eyes and stood slowly.

"We should get going," Carla said.

A lone howl sounded, close by. Maria began to tremble.

"I thought they only hunted at night," she said.

Carla nodded. "Most of them. There have been a few smart ones hunting during the day from the beginning, when humans thought they were safe. Now more and more of them are out in the daylight."

Maria shuddered. "We'll never make it on foot. We're over a mile away. That thing sounded like it was close by."

"We'll make it," Carla replied. "Let's keep moving."

There was a tremendous crash, from the same direction the howl had come. Maria felt the blood drain from her face; looking at Carla, she saw a smile lighting up her features. She reached her hand out to Juan, and he took it.

"Let's go," Carla said.

They only saw one other rambler, and Carla took it out without pausing in her steps. Maria called out to her as the ringing in her ears died down.

"Where did you learn to shoot like that?" she cried.

"A few days ago my world was full of gorgeous monsters," Carla laughed. "I had to be able to hold my own among them. Now only one monster matters."

Maria looked at her, curious. Carla smiled, and pointed.

"There's our boat," she said brightly.

* * *

Maria did not have time to be amazed at how many boats were still docked, floating peacefully in their slips. She didn't have a moment to ask how Carla had gotten a shopping cart onto the deck, or how she had kept it full of supplies from the store to the boat. In the same moment that Carla pointed and spoke, a shot rang out. A man stepped from the shadows, and three others stepped out behind him.

"Well, well, well," he said, cocking his rifle to ready it for another round. "Look at that, boys. I told you they were headed somewhere. It looks like we got ourselves a boat and some food to go along with our pretty new-"

Everyone's eyes were on him as he talked to his men over his shoulder. No one realized that Carla had drawn her weapon until his left eye disappeared in a burst of blood. Before his weapon had clattered to the ground beside his lifeless body, another shot rang out. Another man fell, and the remaining two scattered. Carla turned to Maria.

"Get on the boat!" she yelled. "Get out of here!"

Maria grabbed Juan's hand and yanked; he planted his feet and started wailing as gunfire filled the air. She looked to the men, walking toward her and firing past her; she glanced back at Carla, backing away and firing rounds at them like clockwork. When her clip was exhausted she dropped it in the street, slammed another into place. Carla stopped in the street, pointed her weapon carefully and squeezed off a single shot. One of the men went down with a strangled cry.

"Get out of here!" Carla screamed again.

The last man was taking cover behind an abandoned car, crouched out of sight. Carla jerked her head in the direction of the boat and emptied the clip into the driver's door. Maria didn't see whether the man poked his head up as she heard another clip clacking into place; she grabbed Juan about the waist and tossed him over her shoulders like a sack of potatoes. He struggled and screamed while she ran, and Maria hunkered down as much as she could as more bullets ripped through the air. They made it to the boat, and she ran in the door and dumped him as carefully as possible on the wooden floor.

"Please stay here, sweetie," Maria gasped. She ran back out on deck, grasped the handle of the cart. The gunshots had stopped, and she swept the scene she had left behind with her worried gaze.

"Carla?" she called out, quietly.

Maria's eyes went to a sudden movement, one of the men sitting up in the street. He wasn't a man anymore; the flesh had already begun to fall from his face, and his rusted eyes gleamed with inhuman hunger.

Another shot rang out, and the monster's head exploded. Its body plopped back into the street with a quiet thud. Carla stepped from behind a stranded pickup, clutching her shoulder. She was bleeding. Maria ran to her, wound her arm around her own shoulders and half-carried her to the deck. Carla grabbed the handle of the cart as she passed, tried to bring it inside with her.

Maria shook her head, tears streaming down her face. She pulled, and Carla's fingers came free. Inside the door, she set Carla carefully on the floor next to Juan. She rushed out to get the cart, pulled it inside, and locked the door behind her. Looking around, she saw a trail of blood leading to the cabin. The motor turned over, and she felt the floor lurch under her feet. Maria spread her hands to steady herself and followed the trail of blood.

She knelt beside Carla, took the hand that Juan wasn't holding. There was a puddle of blood on the floor that kept getting bigger; Juan wouldn't take his eyes from it.

"It...drives..." Carla gasped, "like...like a...car..."

"Shhh, sweetie," Maria said through her tears. "I can drive it. We made it. You saved us."

Carla shook her head. "No...listen... important...California...you have to..."

She coughed, and wheezed, and blood trickled from her lip.

"You have to go to California!" she whispered fiercely.

Maria looked at Juan, then back at Carla.

"California? Why? What's in California?"

"The...the cure," Carla gasped. "Promise me!"

"I don't see why-"

"Promise!" Carla whispered. "Please, you have to promise..."

Her chin dropped to her chest, and her labored breathing ceased.

"I promise!" Maria shouted, as if it would bring her back. "I promise, Carla! We'll go to California. I promise, okay?"

She took her in her arms, held her close. Blood stained her clothes, and tears streamed down her face, as she rocked the woman in her arms. After a few moments she stood and looked out at the open sea before them. She glanced at the digital compass, adjusted the wheel until she was satisfied, and dragged the corpse to the door. A slip of stained paper fell from the pocket as the body bumped across the frame. Her eyes came open as Maria kicked her over the side, and Maria saw that they were a rusted red. It wasn't Carla in there any more.

Watching the body disappear beneath the waves, then watching the spot where it had sunk, Maria thought she saw a burst of blood in the water behind them. It was hard to tell, with the shifting waves and the shadows they cast. She went back inside, bending to pick up the bloodstained photo as she passed it. She held it before her as she walked, closing and locking the door behind her. After checking their heading once more, she knelt next to Juan.

"Are you alright, sweetie?" she asked, quietly.

Juan looked at his hand; it was covered in blood.

"Carla's in heaven," Juan said softly.

Fresh tears welled in her eyes.

"That's right, sweetie," Maria said firmly. "Carla's in heaven."

He reached out his bloody hand, and she took it in hers. They sat there for a moment together, each of them lost in their own world.

There was a loud clunk under their feet, and Maria started. Rising slowly, still clutching his hand, she looked out the windshield to see if they had hit something. They hadn't; they were well out to sea, with nothing but water before them. Lowering herself to his side, she started again as he spoke suddenly.

"Daddy's here!" Juan chimed happily. "Daddy's here!"

Dear reader,

Who is Maria's hero? Frank? Carla? Juan?

I've asked myself that question plenty of times. The best I could come up with is that it's all three; if you come up with something a little more clear, let me know. Meanwhile...

This is a kind of epic milestone.

This publication officially marks the end of the 'Year of the Zombie' for me. As fond as I am of many things Eastern, I'm sticking with the Western calendar for theming my life and my writing. By the time you read this, I'll be writing a different story entirely. I'll be in a whole other world, in a way I never have before, and inviting you to take the ride with me...the only zombies in my life will be the ones I use to over-decorate for Halloween every year.

(If that says 'over-decorate', that's my editor at it again; even a thing like a yearly fright fest needs to grow and evolve!)

The wonderful thing is, I don't really have to leave any of this behind. That's the cool thing about writing books; they're always out there for new readers to find and enjoy, and authors get to reconnect with their own characters as those discoveries happen. I love both of those connections every time.

This electronic world has made the campfire storyteller's job way easier as far as reaching people; if I haven't had a chance to meet you, I'd love to hear from you. The story may be told, but you can bet these characters live on in my mind...even the ones that didn't survive the tale itself.

If this is the first of my books that you have read, I hope you find special delight in seeking out the others. For those of you that have been reading these in order, and especially those of you who have read my other books, I have something to say to you.

Thank you so much for taking this journey with me. It has been a sacred path for me to walk, made all the more special for you walking it with me. I hope you stick with me in years to come, and that your love of my books becomes a bridge that gets well worn for all the crossing.

I'll be bringing you something cool and fun and different soon, especially if you are a member of the 'Secret Society of Deeper Meaning'. Right now I want to express my gratitude, and make a recommendation.

Thanks for reading!
All the best,
Jay
Jay@JayNorry.com

ODE TO CHRISTINA MCMULLEN

This is officially the last of the 'Year of the Zombie' publications for me. I have mixed feelings about it, but...time marches on, and the 'Year of the Dreamer' is fast approaching.

I hope you have read all of the 'Zombie Zero' publications, and that you enjoyed every bit of them. You may have noticed, if you did, that one Christina McMullen plays a pretty important part in all of this. The Christina McMullen I write about in the books is a fictional character, of course...but there's another one that exists in real life, and she is the inspiration for the brilliant author and seasteader that exists in 'Zombie Zero'. Now that you've read all of these, I feel safe telling you about her books.

Get ready to go down a very delightful rabbit hole, my friend...

The first book I read by Christina McMullen was 'Kind of Like Life'. I didn't set my expectations too high, and was as ready to ditch the book as I am any other by an author I'm only just discovering. It quickly became clear that was not going to happen.

Not far into the book, it turned a corner that I had not seen coming at all. Since that first revelation, I have read all of her books that I can and plan to read all the rest. If I'm not caught up to everything she has written by now, I hope it's because she wrote more.

When I reached out to her as a fan, Christina McMullen responded graciously. Unlike other heroes I had put in the book, her role was a pivotal one. It was my way of showing that flexible and creative thinking were the best solution to saving the world, and my way of handing that responsibility off to others in the same breath.

She played it cool in her response, and acted like she wasn't prepared for this eventuality. I like to think the Christina McMullen in my books tells a tale that will never happen pretty accurately. With how humble she is about her writing, she may even have a better plan for all this than I did.

For all we know, she may have prevented a zombie outbreak by writing 'Going Green'.

If you're not done getting your zombie fix, that's a great place to start. Juan got to read it before me, in 'Maria's Hero'. I made myself wait until after I had written my own zombie books.

It's a treat I'm looking forward to.

Also available from J.K. Norry. . .

<u>Zombie Zero</u>
Zombie Zero: The First Zombie
Zombie Zero: The Last Zombie

<u>Zombie Zero: The Short Stories</u>
Volume 1: The Sickness Spreads
Volume 2: The Beginning of the End
Volume 3: Love Lost at Sea
Volume 4: The Zombie Killers
Volume 5: Monstrous Consequences
Volume 6: The Heart of the Monster

<u>The Walking Between Worlds trilogy</u>
Demons & Angels (Book I)
Rise of the Walker King (Book II)
Fall of the Walker King (Book III)

<u>Short Stories</u>
Everything Is Broken: A Love Story
Allen's Stride
The Walker's Way

<u>As Jay Norry</u>
Stumbling Backasswards Into the Light

Learn more about the author at
www.JayNorry.com